~Tabby and the Pup~
Prince

Tabby and the Pup Prince

By Mia Bell

Scholastic Inc.

With special thanks to Conrad Mason

Text copyright © 2019 by Working Partners Limited
Cover and interior art copyright © 2019 Scholastic Inc.

All rights reserved. Published by Scholastic Inc., *Publishers since 1920*, 557 Broadway, New York, NY 10012, by arrangement with Working Partners Limited. Series created by Working Partners Limited, London. SCHOLASTIC and associated logos are trademarks and/or registered trademarks of Scholastic Inc. KITTEN KINGDOM is a trademark of Working Partners Limited.

The publisher does not have any control over and does not assume any responsibility for author or third-party websites or their content.

This book is a work of fiction. Names, characters, places, and incidents are either the product of the author's imagination or are used fictitiously, and any resemblance to actual persons, living or dead, business establishments, events, or locales is entirely coincidental.

ISBN 978-1-338-29235-0

10 9 8 7 6 5 4 3 2 1   19 20 21 22 23

Printed in the U.S.A.   40
First printing 2019
Book design by Baily Crawford

Table of Contents

Chapter 1

FETCH!

"Kitties . . . Attention!"

Princess Tabby stood up straight beside her brothers, Felix and Leo. Her tail shook with excitement as Captain Edmund walked back and forth across the playroom.

"Today, kitties, I am going to teach you something very important indeed!" The captain of the guard twirled his whiskers.

He was a big orange tomcat, and his silver armor sparkled with medals.

He must be the bravest soldier in all Mewtopia, thought Tabby. *He defeated the horrible Pigeon of Coo! And the Great Earthworm of Wiggleville!* This was going to be the best lesson ever.

"Now, watch closely..." said Captain Edmund. He had something behind his back. A second later, he held it out with both paws. "Ta da!" Tabby blinked.

"But ... it's a ball," said Tabby's younger brother, Leo. He sounded just as let down as Tabby felt.

"I thought it would be a sword," whispered her older brother, Felix. "What a relief!"

That's just like Felix, thought Tabby with a smile. Her older brother had always been a bit of a scaredy-cat.

"Well noticed, young Leo," said Captain Edmund. "It is, indeed, a ball! A nice, shiny red one. And today, we are going to learn a wonderful game called 'fetch.' First, I throw the ball, like so . . ." Edmund tossed the ball across the floor. "Then I fetch it, like so!" He jumped up and grabbed the ball with his teeth.

"Please, Captain Edmund," said Tabby, "could you teach us some fencing instead?"

"I bet you could fight anyone in all Mewtopia!" said Leo. He took one of Nanny Mittens's brooms and swung it like a sword.

She might have scolded him if she wasn't upstairs taking a long catnap.

Captain Edmund laughed and lifted the broom from Leo's orange paw. "Dear me!" he said, patting Leo on the head. "Why would the royal kittens need to know about sword fighting?"

"You must have heard about King Gorgonzola and his wicked rats," said Felix. His black fur fluffed up with fear. "He tried to steal the magical Golden Scroll!"

"He was going to use it to make his own laws," said Leo.

"Because he wants to rule Mewtopia himself!" added Tabby. "So that's why we should learn to fight. In case he comes back!"

Captain Edmund looked at Tabby. "Ah yes," he said. "I also heard something about three brave young kittens who saved the day ... You haven't heard anything about that, have you?"

Tabby stared hard at her paws so she didn't have to look him in the eye. *We know everything about that*, she thought. *Because we were those kittens!* But they had worn costumes, so no cat in Mewtopia knew the truth.

Every time Tabby thought about the adventure they'd had, her fur stood on end with fear ... and with excitement. *If Gorgonzola tries anything else, we'll be ready for him!*

"Let's stick to fetch," said Captain Edmund. "Just remember, you're royal kittens! We can't have you going off on adventures, pretending to be the Whiskered Wonders, now, can we?"

"Wow . . . the Whiskered Wonders!" said Leo, hopping from paw to paw. "Is that what the kitizens are calling us? I mean, them!"

"It sounds like something from a fairy tale!" said Tabby. She'd read about brave kitty heroes all her life. *And now I am one! A Whiskered Wonder . . .*

"That's enough, now," said Captain Edmund with a frown. "You must all be on your best behavior today. The dog king and queen of Barkshire will be arriving very soon with their son, the pup prince, and a hundred of their doggy citizens."

"We're *always* supposed to be on our best behavior," Leo grumbled. Nanny Mittens only told them so ten times a day.

"This is different, Leo," said Tabby. "Remember what Mom and Dad said? Mewtopia and Barkshire used to fight all the time, and they want to make sure it never happens again."

"That's right, Tabby," said Captain Edmund, nodding. "This visit from the royal hounds could make peace between our kingdoms forever. We must make sure we are polite and kind to all the dogs."

"I've never met a dog before," said Felix, chewing his claws. "They're not scary, are they?"

"Not to me," said Captain Edmund. "But then again, I'm not scared of much. Dogs are just *different* from cats. For example, they don't purr. Instead, they wag their tails."

"No way!" said Leo, swishing his own tail back and forth. Tabby and Felix giggled. "Like this? Are you sure?"

"Very sure," said Captain Edmund. "And instead of mewing, they bark!"

"What's barking?" asked Tabby.

"You'll find out soon, young kitty," said Captain Edmund. "Because you three are going to look after the pup prince. That's

why your parents asked me to teach you fetch. It's his favorite game."

"Boring!" whispered Leo to Tabby. "Anyway, I can hardly move in these silly, fancy clothes, let alone pounce on a ball!"

Tabby sighed and looked down at her dress. It was made of green silk with gold bows. It was the most beautiful thing she had ever worn. *But I'd much rather be wearing our secret costumes!* She and her brothers had made them after their fight with King Gorgonzola, using things from the dress-up box. Tabby's costume was black and loose to make it easier to fight. She had even cut a mask out of red silk so that she could sneak out of the palace without being seen. *Just in case Gorgonzola comes back...*

"Look at our smart little kittens!" purred a familiar voice.

Tabby grinned as Queen Elizapet stepped into the playroom, followed by King Pouncalot. Captain Edmund bowed low.

Tabby's parents were both dressed in their finest red capes and golden crowns. But she could tell from their flicking tails that they were nervous.

"Are you ready, my sweet kittens?" said Queen Elizapet. "They'll be here any minute! Oh, I do hope they're nice. Come with us now—we have something to show you."

"Where are we going?" asked Leo as the three royal kittens followed their parents.

"To the kitchens!" said King Pouncalot. He led the way down a stone staircase. "Today is so important that we are going to be using the Orb of Plenty."

Tabby gasped. "You mean the magical one?"

"That's right," said Queen Elizapet. "We've invited everyone in Mewtopia to meet the royal hounds and their dog citizens. When it's time for the feast, the Orb of Plenty will magically make more of the food our chefs have cooked. Then we can feed everyone!"

"But first," said King Pouncalot, "we want to try it out and make sure it's working."

They stepped through a great arch into the royal kitchens.

A blast of heat hit them at once, along with a thousand wonderful smells. Tabby's belly growled. It was like walking into a huge cave, with copper pots and pans hanging above. Cats in white aprons rushed here and there. They added spices to frying pans, chopped up vegetables, and stirred bubbling pots.

A long wooden table ran down the middle of the kitchen. Tabby saw cat lords and ladies standing around it, purring in delight at something. Tabby's fur stood on end when she saw what it was.

"Look!" whispered Leo, his big yellow eyes wide. "The Orb of Plenty!"

The orb sat on a blue velvet pillow, with soldiers standing behind it. It was no bigger than the ball Captain Edmund had used to play fetch. But it was made of silver as shiny and bright as a mirror. The kitchen fires were reflected on its curved surface.

"We had it brought up from the royal treasure chamber," said King Pouncalot. "Now for the test run. Where did those dog biscuits get to?"

Everyone turned to look around the

kitchen. Felix pointed to a little box of biscuits that had fallen under the table. He was about to speak when Leo clapped a paw over his mouth.

What's he up to? Tabby wondered.

The little orange cat snuck over to the box. Quickly, Leo put the bone-shaped biscuits into his left pocket. Then he dug in his right pocket and dropped something else into the box.

Tabby grinned.

"You'll get us in trouble!" hissed Felix.

But just then, Queen Elizapet spotted the box. "Leo has found it! Well done, Leo! The dogs will love these treats."

The queen carried the box to the middle of the table. She laid one paw on the orb, still holding the box in her other paw.

"Quiet, everyone!" called King Pouncalot.

At once, everyone stopped what they were doing and turned to watch. The only noise came from the fires and the bubbling pots. Tabby held her breath. *We're going to see some real magic!*

Queen Elizapet closed her eyes. Then she spoke softly.

"Orb of Plenty, hear my call.

Show your magic, feed us all!"

The orb began to glow with a blue light. Then gasps came from the lords and ladies. Tabby couldn't believe her eyes! Biscuits were rising up from the box and falling onto the stone floor. *Wait, those aren't biscuits . . .* They were little pink candies with gray swirls. *Tuna treats!*

Tabby caught Leo's eye. He was grinning from ear to ear. *So that's what Leo put in the box . . .*

Queen Elizapet looked in surprise at the pile of candy around her paws. "Do you think something's wrong with the orb?" she asked.

"No," said King Pouncalot. He gave Leo a serious look. "I think something's wrong with *this* little rascal!" He shook his head. "We've told you how important this day is, Leo. This is exactly the sort of trick that might upset the royal hounds. We are counting on you to behave. Understand?"

Leo nodded, his whiskers drooping.

"I told him so!" said Felix.

Tabby was just reaching for a tuna treat, when a trumpet blast sounded through the palace. Her heart began to thump.

"Oh my whiskers, they're here!" cried Queen Elizapet, almost dropping the orb. "Guards, take the orb back to the treasure chamber at once . . . Captain Edmund will guard it there until it's time for the feast. Come, kittens, we must greet our guests!"

Chapter 2

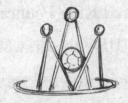

HIDE-AND-SQUEAK

Creeeeak! The drawbridge began to swing open.

Tabby stood whisker to whisker with her brothers. *On the other side of that drawbridge are the dog royals!* she thought. Any moment now, the royal kittens would see them for the first time. Tabby smoothed down her dress.

Queen Elizapet was making sure King

Pouncalot's crown was straight. "Hurry, dear!" whispered King Pouncalot nervously.

Then—*THUMP!*—the drawbridge fell into place. Sun shone into the gatehouse.

"Welcome to Mewtopia!" said King Pouncalot. He stepped forward with his paws wide. Then he stopped.

Four figures were climbing out of a fancy blue carriage with golden wheels and a golden bone painted on the side. But the dogs weren't at all like Tabby thought they would be.

"They look funny," giggled Leo.

"Shh!" hissed Felix.

But Leo was right. The dogs had big eyes, hairy faces, and long noses, just like Tabby had seen in pictures. But the dog king's cloak dragged behind him in the dust. His crown was much too big for him. In fact, all his clothes were!

The three princes with him looked even stranger. Their capes were all ripped. It looked as though they had taken one big cape and torn it into three pieces.

"I thought there was only one pup prince," said Tabby. "And where's the dog queen?"

"And what about all their dog citizens?" Felix added.

"Hush now," said Queen Elizapet. "We must not be rude to our guests!" But she looked confused, too.

The dog king walked across the draw-bridge. "Keep up, you fools!" he growled as the pups ran after him.

"He sounds mean," whispered Leo.

"I heard that!" snapped the dog king. Leo froze. Tabby noticed that his voice squeaked a little. *Maybe he's nervous, too?*

"My son is very sorry," said King Pouncalot, giving Leo a warning look. Then he bowed low. "Welcome to Mewtopia, Your Dogginess! I am King Pouncalot, and this is Queen Elizapet. Felix, Tabby, and Leo are our royal kittens."

Tabby curtsied while her brothers bowed. But the dog king just nodded quickly. "Yes,

yes, hello. This is, er . . . Prince Hairy, Prince Smelly, and Prince Fleabag."

What weird names, thought Tabby.

"May we take your cloaks?" asked Queen Elizapet.

"No!" said the dog king, shaking his head so hard that it wiggled in a funny way.

Tabby frowned. The dog royals seemed very weird indeed. But she remembered what Captain Edmund had said. *Dogs are just different from cats.*

"Not to worry," said Queen Elizapet. "Will your dog citizens be coming soon?"

"No," snapped the dog king. "They aren't coming anymore."

"Oh, that's too bad," said King Pouncalot.

"But I'm sure we will still have a wonderful day. If you will just come this way . . ." He led the dog royals through a door into a long hall with a red carpet. Huge paintings of catkings and catqueens hung on the walls. Soldiers stood at every door.

"The palace seems well guarded," said the dog king. He stared at the guards' silver swords.

"Oh yes," said King Pouncalot. "Perhaps you've heard of the wicked rat, King Gorgonzola? He tried to steal our Golden Scroll!"

"And almost got away with it," said the dog king. "He must be very smart."

"Not as smart as the Whiskered Wonders!" said Leo.

The dog king narrowed his eyes. "You must be worried about your other treasures now," he said. "Like the Orb of Plenty . . . where are you keeping it?"

Tabby heard a giggle. *Was that the pup princes?* Tabby wondered. She frowned at them, and they all got quiet and looked away.

"Don't worry," said Queen Elizapet. "The Orb of Plenty is safe in our treasure chamber. Captain Edmund is guarding it. He's the best soldier in Mewtopia!"

"Now," said King Pouncalot, stopping outside the throne room. "Why don't we show His Dogginess around the palace, while you kitties and pups play together?"

Do we have to? thought Tabby. But she smiled and flicked her ears. "Yes, Dad." *If we don't behave, Mom and Dad might not be able to make peace with Barkshire!*

The royal kittens ran off, followed by the pups.

"You'll love it here," said Felix. "We've got extra treats today. Normally we have sour lemon sardines and trout twisters, but the chefs have made some special dog biscuits for you!"

"Yuck," said Prince Hairy. "Dog biscuits make me sick!"

"Give me a nice smelly lump of cheese any day!" said Prince Fleabag.

The pups all nodded. Once again, Tabby

was sure their heads wiggled. She frowned, but said nothing. *I can't be rude. That's what Mom said! But she also said that dogs love these biscuits . . .*

They climbed up a twisting staircase and came out in the playroom. There were boxes everywhere, piled high with squeaky toys made just for the puppies, but they didn't seem at all interested. Instead they just sat in a row, looking bored.

"Let's play fencing!" said Leo. He picked up the broom again.

"Or we could pretend to be explorers," said Felix. "That might be safer. Look, I'll make a ship!" He dragged some pillows across the floor and began to stack them.

"Or we could try on suits of armor," said Tabby.

"Don't you have anything fun to do?" asked Prince Smelly.

They're just as mean as their dad! thought Tabby. But she ignored it and picked up the red ball Captain Edmund had given them. "I know—let's play fetch!" She threw it up with one paw and caught it again.

The puppies just stared at her. "What's fetch?" said Prince Hairy.

Tabby, Leo, and Felix looked at one another with wide eyes. *This doesn't make any sense,* thought Tabby. *Captain Edmund said the pup prince loved fetch! He must have been wrong.*

"What *should* we do, then?" asked Felix.

The puppies whispered to one another. At last they looked up. "We've got an idea," said Prince Fleabag. "Let's play hide-and-squeak."

Leo stroked his whiskers. "Do you mean hide-and-*seek*?"

"That's what I said!" snapped Prince Fleabag. "You kitties hide first. Then we'll come and find you."

Tabby thought the puppies looked meaner than ever. *But at least we found something they want to do!* She sighed. "Okay. Close your eyes and count to a hundred . . ."

The puppies all turned to the wall, and the royal kittens raced out of the playroom.

Tabby ran down the stairs. *Where can I*

hide . . . ? She could sneak behind the royal milk freezer. Or go behind the curtains in the library. She could even curl up under her dad's desk . . . Then she stopped. The puppies didn't know the palace, and she was supposed to be looking after them. *I should choose somewhere they can find us easily*, she thought. She ran down the hall and hid behind a suit of armor. She squeezed up against the wall, panting.

It was dark and quiet in the hall, and there were spiderwebs in every corner. Tabby waited and waited. But no one came. *Where have those puppies gone?*

After a while, she noticed a weird noise from close by. A low growl. Then another one. And another. *Maybe it's barking! Captain Edmund never told us what it sounded like.* Tabby froze, her whiskers shaking, trying not to make even the smallest sound.

Then she heard something else. Paws coming down the hall.

Slowly, Tabby looked around the suit of armor. It was Felix and Leo, tip-pawing along.

Tabby grinned and jumped out. "Boo!"

Felix and Leo jumped, too. "Tabby!" said Felix. "You scared me!"

"Not me," said Leo, but his fur had puffed up all over.

"Why aren't you hiding?" asked Tabby.

"We were," said Leo. "But the puppies

didn't find us. They're really bad at this game! Then we heard a funny growling sound."

"Did you hear it, too?" asked Felix.

Tabby nodded. "I think it came from that way . . ."

Together, the three royal kittens walked along the dark hall. Then they turned the corner. Tabby gasped. "It's Captain Edmund!"

The big tomcat was curled up beside an old wooden door. *The door to the treasure chamber!* He was fast asleep, and his silver armor gently rose and fell.

"That's not growling," said Leo. "It's snoring!"

A shiver ran through Tabby, right to the

tip of her tail. "I don't like this . . ." she said. "Captain Edmund never falls asleep when he's working!"

Felix ran over and shook the captain. The orange cat opened his eyes. Then, suddenly, he sat up, blinking. "What happened?" he said. "Where am I?"

"You were guarding the treasure chamber, remember?" said Leo, hopping from paw to paw.

"But you fell asleep!" said Tabby.

Captain Edmund stood up quickly. His tail flicked nervously. "Thank goodness you woke me. Come on—we have to make sure the Orb of Plenty is still safe!"

Chapter 3

THOSE RATTY RASCALS

The treasure chamber was just as amazing as Tabby remembered. Piles of gold, silver, and jewels lay all around, lit by glowing torches hung from the walls. Tabby spotted the Golden Scroll on its stone stand. *But where's the Orb of Plenty...?*

"Look!" said Felix, pointing. Tabby let out a sigh of relief. The orb sat on its deep-blue pillow in the corner, just as shiny and silver as before.

"Oh my whiskers!" said Captain Edmund, puffing out his cheeks. "What a relief . . ."

Just then, King Pouncalot and Queen Elizapet hurried into the room.

"Have you seen him?" asked King Pouncalot. "Have you seen the dog king?"

Felix frowned. "We thought he was with you!"

"He was," said Queen Elizapet, throwing her paws up sadly. "He asked us what catnaps were. Then he wanted us to show him. So, we curled up and closed our eyes—"

"And when we opened them again, he was gone!" finished King Pouncalot. He scratched his head, staring at the royal kittens. "Hold on. Where did the pup princes go?"

Tabby gave her brothers a worried look. "Sorry, Dad . . . they wanted to play hide-and-seek."

"They're probably still looking for us," said Leo. "Maybe."

"Hopefully," said Felix.

"Why don't you tell the guards to announce that the feast is ready?" said Captain Edmund. "Wherever the royal hounds have gone, they will hear the dinner bell and come back."

"What a good idea!" cried Queen Elizapet. "Come along, my dear, let's go. Captain

Edmund, would you mind taking the orb down to the kitchens?"

"Not at all." Captain Edmund bowed.

"We can come, too," said Tabby. "Maybe that's where the pup princes have hidden. They might have been looking for cheese to eat . . ."

The Royal Kittens ran out of the Great Hall, down the stairs, and into the kitchens. Cooks were rushing everywhere. "Here it comes!" said one. Tabby turned to see Captain Edmund bring in the Orb of Plenty. He gently placed it on the table, among silver dishes full of dog biscuits, bone-shaped cakes, and fish pie.

"Prince Hairy?" Tabby called. She crawled under the table, but she couldn't see the puppies.

"Prince Smelly? Are you in there? Prince Fleabag?" called Felix. He looked in the food cupboards, while Leo searched inside the big copper pots on the shelves.

It's like they disappeared! Tabby was just about to give up, when she heard Captain Edmund cry out.

"It's not working!"

Tabby ran out from under the table. Captain Edmund was holding up the orb, staring at it and looking confused.

"Try it again!" said a cook.

With one paw on a big pile of dog

biscuits, and the other holding the orb, Captain Edmund said:

"*Orb of Plenty, hear my call.*

Show your magic, feed us all!"

But there was no blue light. No magic at all. The pile of dog biscuits stayed just the same size. All around, the cooks began to whisper to one another in fear.

"I don't understand!" said Captain Edmund. He looked closely at the orb. "Something must be wrong with it. Now we will never have enough food for the feast! The dog king will think it's some kind of trick, and we will lose our chance at peace with Barkshire!"

Felix began to chew his claws again. "I don't like this," he said.

"Do you think someone broke the orb on purpose?" asked Tabby.

"But who would do that?" asked Leo.

The three kittens all spoke at the same time. "King Gorgonzola!"

Captain Edmund looked up sharply. His nose twitched back and forth. "Wait! King

Gorgonzola . . . Tickle my whiskers, I'm sure I just saw him . . ."

"Oh no!" Tabby gasped. "Was it outside the treasure chamber? When you fell asleep?"

Captain Edmund nodded slowly. "Yes, that's it. I thought it was just a bad dream. But maybe he really was there . . ."

Tabby took the Orb of Plenty from Captain Edmund and ran a claw over it. *There!* She found the edge of something and lifted gently. Tabby could hardly breathe as she opened the orb like a present. Inside was something round and yellow.

"That's not silver!" said Captain Edmund, pointing at the wrapping. "It's just tinfoil!"

"And this isn't a magical orb," said Tabby. She held up the yellow ball. "It's just cheese!"

Cooks crowded around, whispering in shock.

"She's right," said Captain Edmund. "Leaping fleas, we've been tricked! This is a fake orb!"

"I bet it was King Gorgonzola!" said Felix. "He must have snuck up on Captain Edmund. Then he stole the Orb of Plenty and switched it for this fake one."

"Of course!" said Leo. "He loves cheese."

Just then, they heard a blast of trumpets from the palace gates.

Everyone looked at one another, their faces confused.

"I don't understand," said Felix, frowning. "That's not the dinner bell."

"That's the sound for the royal hounds arrival," said Leo.

"But they already *have* arrived!" said Captain Edmund.

"Unless . . ." said Tabby. "Unless they weren't the dog royals at all!"

"What do you mean?" asked Leo, whiskers shaking.

Tabby gasped. "King Gorgonzola isn't the only one who loves cheese. Those pup princes do, too. In fact, I don't think they were pups at all!" Tabby cried. "I think they must have been Gorgonzola's horrible rat servants!"

"And if those pups were really rats," said Felix, "then so was the dog king. He was King Gorgonzola all along!" The cooks all gasped. Captain Edmund clapped a paw to his mouth.

"No wonder their clothes didn't fit," said Tabby. "And no wonder their heads wiggled. They were just masks. The dog royals were just rats in doggy *costumes*!"

The royal kittens stared at one another in fear. *I can't believe King Gorgonzola is back!* thought Tabby.

"Those ratty rascals!" said Captain Edmund. "I must tell your parents right now."

"We should come with you," said Felix

nervously. "The real dog royals are here now, after all, and we have to say hello."

Quickly, Tabby wrapped up the ball of cheese again and stuffed it in her skirts. Then the royal kittens followed Captain Edmund as he ran through the halls.

Tabby's tail flicked with worry. *With no Orb of Plenty, the feast can't happen. The dog royals will be angry, and they might not want to make peace!* That was bad enough. But now King Gorgonzola had the orb himself . . . *What is he planning to do with it?*

Chapter 4

THE PUP PRINCE

"So it's true," said King Pouncalot, walking back and forth. "Gorgonzola is back again!" Captain Edmund and the royal kittens had just finished telling him their story.

"I'll find him, Your Highness," said Captain Edmund. "And the Orb of Plenty, too!"

"No time for that," said Queen Elizapet as the trumpets blasted again. "We have to welcome our guests. No one say anything to them about the missing orb!" Her tail was twitching even more nervously than it had been that morning.

The drawbridge came down with a *thump!*

This time, Tabby saw three dogs climbing out of an old black carriage. They came across the drawbridge with their tails wagging and their pink tongues hanging out. There was the dog king, the dog queen, and just one pup prince. *They look a little like the fake dogs,* Tabby thought. *Except their heads don't wiggle. And their clothes fit. And they look much nicer!*

"Your Majesties," said the dog king. He

bowed low. "Please forgive us! We are so very late."

"Someone stole our carriage," said the dog queen. "It took some time to find a new one."

"The odd thing is, we thought we saw our carriage again just now," said the dog king. "It was racing away from this palace very quickly."

"Was it blue with golden wheels?" asked Leo.

The dog king frowned. "How did you know?"

"Oh, just a guess!" said Felix.

Uh-oh, thought Tabby. *Gorgonzola and his*

rats must have escaped in the carriage! We have to go after him—and fast!

"You've had an awful journey," said Queen Elizapet. "But we're so happy to have you in Mewtopia! I am Queen Elizapet, and this is King Pouncalot. And these are the royal kittens, Tabby, Felix, and Leo."

"Are your doggy citizens coming, too?" asked King Pouncalot.

"Yes, in fact, we already dropped them off in town so that they can make friends with your kitizens." The dog queen smiled.

"Wonderful! May we show you around the palace?" asked King Pouncalot.

"We would love that!" said the dog king.

His tail was wagging faster now. "I am King Rover. This is Queen Ginger and our son, Prince Buddy."

"Do you want to see our playroom?" Felix asked the pup prince.

Buddy bounced up and down, panting with excitement. He had silky golden fur and wore a fancy blue outfit. Tabby thought he looked about the same age as Leo. "Oooh, yes, please! I love playing! And I love play-rooms! Let's go!"

Tabby was disappointed. *We should be going after King Gorgonzola!* But she knew they had to look after Prince Buddy, too. "Come on, then," she said.

The three royal kittens led the puppy

through the palace, up the spiral stairs to their playroom.

"What should we play?" asked Buddy when they reached the top of the stairs. "I know lots of games. And I like them all!"

At least the real pup prince was a lot more fun than those rats were. "How about fetch?" Tabby said.

Buddy's eyes grew wide, and he ran around and around in a circle, chasing his tail. "I love fetch! Fetch is my favorite game ever! I play it all the time!" Suddenly, he stopped and stared into space.

"Is he all right?" whispered Felix.

"I think he's just thinking," Tabby whispered back.

"I've got an idea!" said Buddy suddenly.
"Why don't we pretend to be the Whiskered
Wonders? My nanny, Bernard, told me all
about them. They saved Mewtopia from the
wicked King Gorgonzola, didn't they? Oooh,
I wish I could be a hero just like them! Hey,
is that your playroom? Last one there is a
scared little poodle!"

The royal kittens smiled at one another as the puppy ran off.

"Are you thinking what I'm thinking?" said Tabby.

"Definitely!" said Leo, his big yellow eyes wide. "I can't believe they've heard of us in Barkshire, too! We're famous!"

"No!" said Tabby. "I was thinking we need to get out of here and stop King Gorgonzola. We can't let him escape with the Orb of Plenty."

"But Mom and Dad told us to look after Prince Buddy," said Felix, looking into the playroom. "And we can't take him with us!"

"I have an idea," said Tabby. She ran into the playroom, followed by her brothers.

Buddy had jumped into a box and was digging out toys. His back legs and tail waved in the air.

"Would you like a bone to chew?" asked Tabby.

"No, thanks!" called Buddy from inside the box. "I'm playing!"

"How about a nap?" tried Felix. "There are some really comfy pillows here."

"What's a nap?" asked the puppy.

Leo rolled his eyes. "We'll never get rid of him!"

Unless... "I know," said Tabby. "How about a game of hide-and-seek?"

Buddy's head popped out. His ears stood up straight. "That sounds REALLY COOL!"

"Great!" said Tabby. "We'll count. You—"

But before she could finish, Buddy had raced through the door. "You'll never find me!" he called.

"That was easier than I thought," said Felix.

The kittens waited until they were sure the puppy had hidden. Then they snuck out of the playroom and ran up to their bedroom. Leo opened the dress-up box.

"No time to change!" said Tabby. "Let's just wear our masks, gloves, and capes over our clothes."

Quickly, she tied on her red silk mask. Felix put on his purple one, while Leo tied on the green mask he had made out of his old blanket. Then they threw their long capes over their fine clothes and hid their swords underneath.

"What about Buddy?" said Felix.

Tabby felt sad for the little puppy hiding on his own. *We should be looking after him.* But she knew he would be safer in the palace. "We can worry about him later," she said. "Right now, it's time to save Mewtopia!"

Chapter 5

MAGIC CHEESE

The royal kittens tip-pawed through the palace. Tabby felt her nose twitch with excitement about wearing their new masks for the very first time. *We're the Whiskered Wonders, and now we look like heroes!* The thought of facing King Gorgonzola again was scary . . . but she tried not to think about that.

They went through a heavy wooden door

that the servants used. It was a sunny, windy day outside. *A perfect day to play!* thought Tabby. *But we have a job to do.*

"Now, let's see if we can find those horrible rats," said Tabby.

The royal kittens ran into the stone streets of the village, looking out for rats and a blue carriage. They stuck to quiet, dark alleys. But now and then, Tabby could see the Royal Avenue. It was filled with kitizens and dogs, all talking and laughing, dressed up in their best clothes.

"Look, everybody is making friends!" said Felix happily.

Tabby saw that some cats were busy setting up a very long table in the middle of the road. *The feast must go all the way down the Royal Avenue!* She thought of the Orb of Plenty. If they didn't get it back, there would be no feast and nothing for the kitizens and dogs to eat. Would everyone still get along then?

The kittens ran faster through the village. Above the rooftops, Tabby saw the misty shape of a mountain rising toward the blue sky. *Mount Claw.* After their first adventure as the Whiskered Wonders, the kittens had begged Nanny Mittens to tell them more about the rats and their underground kingdom, Rottingham. She had finally agreed, and she told them that the rats all used to live under Mount Claw.

Over time, King Gorgonzola had made their kingdom bigger and bigger. *Now it goes all the way to the mines beneath Mewtopia*, Tabby remembered.

"Look!" said Leo, pointing down at the stone street.

They had just turned around a corner, and in front of them was a pile of clothes. Tabby blinked. *Wait . . . the clothes are snoring!* "It's a cat," she whispered as they came closer. "But he's asleep."

"There's another one!" said Felix, pointing to a Siamese cat curled against a wall.

"There's a sleeping dog over there, too," said Leo. "What do you think is going on?"

"It's just like Captain Edmund," said

Tabby. "He fell asleep when King Gorgonzola came to steal the orb. But Captain Edmund never falls asleep . . ."

"So maybe Gorgonzola did something to put him to sleep!" Leo cried.

"Maybe Gorgonzola has put these cats and dogs to sleep, too!" said Felix.

"That means we're on the right track," said Tabby. "We just have to follow the sleeping kitizens and dogs!"

"Wait," said Felix. He stopped. His ears went up, and his whiskers twitched. "Do you hear something?"

"I hear snoring," said Leo.

Felix shook his head. "Not that! There's

something else." He froze for a moment. Then he suddenly spun around. "Ha!"

Tabby turned just in time to see someone move away through the shadows.

"Someone's following us!" Leo gasped. "Probably one of Gorgonzola's mean rats. I bet they're going to sneak up on us and try to make us fall asleep, too!"

"What should we do?" asked Felix, chewing his claws nervously.

"I know," said Tabby. "Let's pretend we didn't see them. Then we can hide and pounce on them when they get close!"

"I like the sound of that!" said Leo, grinning.

The three royal kittens kept walking down the street. They went around a corner, then Tabby flicked her ears to give the signal. Quickly, they all ran into a dark little alley. They sat, watching the road and waiting. *Maybe it's King Gorgonzola*, thought Tabby nervously. *Or one of his nasty rat servants . . .*

Leo wrinkled his nose. "What's that funny smell?" he whispered.

Felix sniffed. "I think it's cheese!"

They looked down. Lying there in the shadows was a big yellow lump of cheese. Tabby took off her glove and picked it up. "It really does smell very cheesy," she whispered. Her head began to feel heavy. Her eyes closed. *Maybe I'll just take a little catnap,* she thought. *Those stones look so cool and comfy . . .*

"Tabby!" hissed Felix.

Tabby blinked. She dropped the cheese. As soon as it left her paw, her sleepiness was gone. "Wow!" She gasped. "I think it must be this cheese that made everyone fall asleep!"

"It must be magic or something," said Leo. "King Gorgonzola probably brought it with him. We're lucky that our masks are covering our noses, or we'd probably be asleep already. And look! There's more cheese over there."

The crumbs of cheese led farther down the alley, disappearing into darkness.

"Someone's coming!" Felix whispered suddenly.

The royal kittens ducked into a dark doorway and watched the road. *Now we'll see who's following us*, thought Tabby. She held her breath, ready to pounce.

Then someone stepped into view. Someone with silky golden fur and a fancy blue outfit . . .

"Is that who I think it is?" said Leo.

Tabby couldn't believe her eyes. *It's Prince Buddy!* He walked carefully. But he was panting, and his tail was wagging.

"Oh my whiskers!" cried Felix. "What if King Gorgonzola kidnaps him? We need to get him back to the palace!"

There's only one thing to do. Tabby stepped out of the alley. "Stop!" she said, holding up a paw. "In the name of the Whiskered Wonders!"

The pup prince jumped in shock. His ears stuck straight up. His eyes grew wide. Then he gasped. "Biscuits and bones, it's the Whiskered Wonders! You're my heroes. Wow, I can't believe you're here! And I'm here, too! I was supposed to be hiding from the royal kittens back in the palace. But they didn't find me, so I sniffed them out. I love smelling things! And I'm good at it. So I followed them all the way here. You smell kind of like them . . . wait!"

He stopped and stared into space, his nose twitching fast.

"It looks like he's thinking again," said Leo.

Buddy's jaw dropped. "You smell *exactly* like the royal kittens! Which means . . . which means . . ."

The pup prince's ears flopped. His tail stopped wagging. Then he rolled over on his back, paws sticking up in the air. In an instant, he was snoring loudly, and his tongue hung out of his mouth.

"Oh no!" cried Tabby "He's fallen asleep!"

Chapter 6

THE FOURTH WONDER

"It's the cheese!" said Felix. "That's why he fell asleep." He pointed to a big lump lying nearby.

"Poor Buddy," said Tabby. "He isn't wearing a mask like us."

"Besides, Buddy loves to sniff things." Felix added.

"So now can we go and catch Gorgonzola?" asked Leo.

Tabby shook her head. "We can't leave Buddy here. We have to take care of him. If something happens to him, the dog royals will never forgive us!"

The royal kittens were quiet, all thinking hard.

"Got it!" said Tabby, at last. "Let's take him to Clawdia! We aren't far from her place." Clawdia was the goldsmith's daughter, who had helped them on their first adventure. *And she's the only cat in the kingdom who knows we're the Whiskered Wonders!*

"Good thinking!" said Felix.

A few minutes later, Tabby knocked on the door of the royal goldsmith's shop.

"Oof!" said Leo, wiping his brow. "Buddy is heavier than he looks!"

Buddy lay on the stones beside them, where they had put him down. His tongue still hung out of his mouth, and he was still snoring loudly.

The door opened, and Tabby grinned. "Hi, Clawdia!"

The goldsmith's daughter was a little black-and-brown cat with a circle of white fur around one eye. Today she was wearing a pretty red dress and a yellow scarf.

"Is your dad here?" Felix whispered.

Clawdia frowned at them. "No, he's at the street party. The shop is closed today. Who are you?"

"It's us, Clawdia!" said Leo, pulling down his mask.

Clawdia peered closer, then gasped. "Your Majesties!" she said. "Wow, it's good to see you again. Is everything all right?" Then she spotted the puppy, and her fur stood on end. "What's that?!"

"He's a puppy," said Tabby. "And he's a prince! We really need to wake him up. If we don't, there might never be peace between Barkshire and Mewtopia ever again!"

"Leaping fleas!" gasped Clawdia. "Come in, come in!"

Clawdia helped the royal kittens lift the puppy through the door. They carried him

to the counter and laid him flat on top. His paws twitched, but he kept on sleeping.

"I've never seen a dog before," said Clawdia. "He looks so funny! His nose is so long. And his ears are so floppy!"

"What now?" asked Felix.

"Maybe we should tickle his belly?" said Clawdia. "Dad told me dogs like that."

"Like this?" said Leo. He tickled Buddy on his tummy.

The pup prince snorted. He blinked, then rolled over and stood on the counter, wide awake. "Hello!" he said. "What's happening? Where am I? Are there any biscuits?" Then he saw the royal kittens. "Oh my, it's the Whiskered Wonders! But you smell exactly like . . ."

"The royal kittens," Tabby said. "That's right, Your Dogginess. That's because we *are* the royal kittens!"

Buddy's ears went up in surprise. "I don't believe it! I'm friends with the Whiskered Wonders?!"

"It's true," said Tabby. "But you have to

keep it secret! Right now, we're chasing the wicked rat, King Gorgonzola. He stole the magical Orb of Plenty, and we're going to get it back. We're following the crumbs of cheese. That's what made you fall asleep—he's put some kind of spell on it!"

"Oh, please, can I come?" Buddy begged. "I've got whiskers! I could be the fourth Wonder!"

Felix flicked his tail nervously. "I don't know about this," he whispered to the other kittens. "What if he gets hurt?"

"I bet he's not as good at fencing as we are," whispered Leo.

"I think we should give him a chance," said Tabby, softly, thinking about how scared she was on their first adventure. "We already know he's brave. And that's the most important thing, isn't it?"

Felix and Leo looked at each other. Then they nodded.

"Oh, thank you, thank you, thank you!" cried Buddy. He leaped down and ran around the shop, chasing his tail.

"Clawdia, can we please borrow your scarf?" asked Tabby. "We need to make a mask for Buddy so Gorgonzola's cheese won't make him fall asleep again."

"Of course!" Clawdia took off her scarf and handed it over. "I'll go to the palace. Someone should tell the king and queen that the Whiskered Wonders are on the case."

"Thanks, Clawdia," said Tabby. "And make sure to cover your nose!"

"It's happening again," said Leo. "We're having another adventure!"

Tabby put a paw on her sword. *We're coming for you, Gorgonzola!*

Chapter 7

A MOST BRILLIANT PLAN

They walked off with Buddy, who was proudly wearing his new yellow mask.

Follow the crumbs of cheese, thought Tabby as they wound their way through the streets. Dogs and cats were curled up here and there along the way, snoring as they dreamed.

"We should pick up the crumbs as we go so they can't put anyone else to sleep," she said.

The crumbs led them down a dark alley and out into a meadow. Soon the sounds of the village were far away. They dropped the crumbs they had found in a puddle of mud and covered them up. More cheese lay on a rocky path through the meadow. The path of cheese went up a hill, then down the other side. But at the bottom of the hill, it stopped.

"Where's the cheese?" said Felix, frowning hard. "I don't see any more."

"Maybe Gorgonzola ate the rest," said Leo.

"I can't see it," said Buddy. "But I can smell it!" His shiny black nose sniffed the air.

Of course! thought Tabby. *Buddy sniffed us*

out when we were playing hide-and-seek. Maybe he can sniff out Gorgonzola, too . . .

"Follow your nose, Your Dogginess," said Tabby. "Do you think you can lead us to the smelly cheese?"

Buddy nodded, his tail wagging hard. "I can do it! I know I can!"

"Just be careful not to sniff too much," said Felix. "We don't want you falling asleep again!"

The pup prince lifted his nose and sniffed the air. Then he began to run.

"It's working!" Tabby grinned.

The royal kittens followed the puppy. He led them across a river and over a small rocky hill, sniffing all the way.

We are almost at Mount Claw! thought Tabby, staring up at the gray mountain above them. It looked like a sharp, curved claw, and it cast a long, dark shadow. *Is that where Gorgonzola has gone?*

Sure enough, Buddy began to sniff his way up the side of the mountain. The royal kittens followed, jumping from rock to rock.

Halfway up the mountain was a small forest, with trees growing among the rocks. The royal kittens were almost through it when Leo cried out, "Ouch!"

"Are you okay?" asked Tabby.

Leo rubbed his head. "Something hit me. I think it came from the trees."

"What could—Ouch!" cried Felix.

Something round and yellow hit him on the head. It bounced off and rolled past Tabby's paws. Tabby stared down at it. *Uh-oh . . .* "It's a big ball of smelly cheese!"

"Take that, nosy kitties!" called a voice from above.

Tabby looked up. Three rats were dancing around at the edge of the forest, each with a bandana tied over their nose. They were juggling balls of cheese and throwing them down the hill.

"It's Brie!" Leo gasped.

"And Chedd!" said Tabby.

"And Mozz!" added Felix. "Gorgonzola's rat servants!"

"Look," said Tabby. "They're still wearing those baggy clothes."

"That's my cape!" said Buddy. "They've torn it in three!" He stopped to sniff at one of the rolling balls of cheese. "Ooh!" he said. "This looks yummy."

"Careful!" said Tabby. She picked up the cheese and threw it away. "Don't get too close, or you'll fall asleep!"

"Look out!" yelled Felix.

The royal kittens hid behind a big tree as the rats threw more cheese. Tabby pulled Buddy along.

"Let's get them!" said Leo.

"But how?" said Felix. "We can't get close while they keep throwing cheese down at us!"

"I know," said Tabby. "We can climb up into the trees! If we jump from tree to tree, we can climb without the cheese hitting us!"

They were just starting to climb up a tree trunk when Tabby heard a little sigh from below. She looked around and saw Buddy staring up sadly.

"I'm sorry," he said. "But dogs can't climb trees! Or I can't, anyway. Maybe I can't be a Whiskered Wonder after all." His head hung low.

"Don't be silly," said Tabby. "I know! We'll distract them. Then you come running out and scare them off. What do you think?"

Buddy's ears perked up again. "That's a good idea! Just wait. I'll be so scary!"

"Great," said Tabby. "Let's go!"

The royal kittens climbed up to the tree-top. Tabby stood on a branch, balancing with her tail. Then she jumped to the next tree.

"Where did they go?" said Brie from below. "I want to throw more cheese at them!"

Looking around, Tabby saw Felix and Leo jumping through the trees on either side. She pointed to a big tree at the very edge of the forest. Then she flicked her ears to give the signal. They all jumped into the branches of the big tree. *There!* Tabby saw the rats below, each carrying a pair of cheese balls in their claws.

"Up here!" yelled Tabby.

All three rats looked up and saw the royal kittens.

"Get them!" called Mozz.

Tabby ducked as the rats began to throw cheese again. *Whoosh!* One ball went high above her head. *Splat!* Another hit a branch.

"Where's that puppy?" yelled Felix.

"Now!" Tabby called back through the forest. "Come on, Buddy!"

She heard a thumping of paws on the ground. Then Buddy came running through the bushes, showing off his long teeth. "Ruff!" he said. "RUFF, RUFF!"

Tabby felt her back arch in fear. *Is that what barking sounds like? It's so loud!*

"It's a monster!" yelled Chedd.

"It's a dog, you fool!" said Mozz.

"I don't like it!" said Brie. "Run for your lives!"

The three rats dropped their cheese. Then they ran, racing away up the mountain.

The pup prince stopped. When he turned around, his teeth were gone, hidden by his long, pink tongue. His tail was wagging. He was just a puppy again.

Tabby felt herself relax. She, Felix, and Leo dropped down from the tree and landed on all fours.

"You did it!" said Leo. "Nice work."

"You were really scary!" Tabby said.

Buddy tucked in his tail, looking shy. "It was nothing, really . . ." he whispered.

"Nonsense—you're a hero!" said Felix, giving the pup prince a high paw. "Now, come on, Wonders. To the top of the mountain!"

Soon, they could all smell cheese. And the more they climbed, the cheesier it got. They were close to the top now, and they were all tired and panting through their mouths so they wouldn't breathe in the powerful smell.

"What do you think Gorgonzola is up to?" wondered Leo.

"We'll find out soon," said Tabby as bravely as she could.

Just then, they climbed around a big rock and saw the very top of the mountain.

Leaping fleas!

Tabby could hardly believe what she saw. Standing there, on a big flat rock, was a huge stone bowl full of melted cheese. It was as big as the milk fountain in the village square, and it bubbled and smoked like a volcano. It was so hot Tabby could feel the heat through her fur.

"Gross!" Felix gasped, holding his nose. "That stinks!"

Even the masks aren't stopping the smell! thought Tabby.

Then a figure stepped out from behind the stone bowl. It was a tall rat with slimy fur, wearing a long black cape and an iron crown, with a black rag tied around his nose. Tabby froze. *It's him!*

"So, we meet again!" said King Gorgonzola. "Those silly masks don't fool me, you know." He took something from inside his cape and held it up. *The Orb of Plenty!*

"It's the orb!" whispered Leo. "I knew it!"

"You're probably wondering what my most brilliant plan is," King Gorgonzola said. "I'm sure you're much too silly to have guessed. You see, I have discovered a special type of cheese that puts you to sleep when you smell it. With the Orb of Plenty,

I can make as much smelly, melty, sleepy cheese as I want! I'm going to make so much, it will spill out and flow down the mountain! I'll flood the whole of Mewtopia . . . with cheese!"

"Uh-oh," whispered Felix. "That sounds awful!"

"Then all the kitizens will fall asleep," Gorgonzola went on. "And there will be so much cheese everywhere, they will never wake up. At last, the kingdom will be mine . . ."

Tabby shook with fear as she imagined what would happen if Gorgonzola's plan worked. The whole kingdom would be asleep. No one would be able to stop the evil rat from doing whatever he wanted. Nobody except . . . *The Whiskered Wonders!*

"I don't think so!" said Tabby. King Gorgonzola stared at her. His eyes were filled with anger. *I forgot how scary Gorgonzola is!* "I mean . . ." she mumbled. "Er . . ."

Then Buddy stepped up beside her. "You should watch out, you naughty rat! You're talking to the Whiskered Wonders!"

"Right!" said Leo, swishing his sword around. "If you are not careful, you'll come to a cheesy end!"

"It's *you* who will get the cheesy end!" yelled King Gorgonzola with an awful, squeaking laugh.

Chapter 8

CHEESECAKE

King Gorgonzola closed his eyes. He laid a claw on the edge of the stone bowl. Then he began to whisper a spell.

"Orb of Plenty, pretty, pretty please,

Cover Mewtopia in stinky cheese!"

The orb glowed blue. Cheese bubbled and spilled over the edge. Tabby watched in horror as it flowed down the side of the bowl and ran between the rocks.

The rat king threw his head back and laughed again.

Gorgonzola looked scarier than ever, but Tabby felt brave with her brothers and Buddy standing beside her. "Quick!" she shouted. "We have to stop him!"

She pulled out her sword and ran forward. But before she could reach King Gorgonzola, his three rat servants came out from behind the big stone bowl. They were still wearing the bandanas over their noses.

"You thought you had gotten rid of us, didn't you?" giggled Brie. She pulled out a rusty old sword. Chedd and Mozz did the same.

Now I really wish Captain Edmund had given us that fencing lesson...

Tabby tried to pretend she was a hero from one of her storybooks. "Stand back!" she said. But Brie just ran forward, waving her sword.

Clang! Tabby's sword hit Brie's.

"Yaaaah!" Mozz and Chedd yelled.

"For Mewtopia!" Leo and Felix ran to meet them.

The air filled with the clanging of swords as the royal kittens fought the rat servants. Tabby ducked as Brie swung at her. She pointed her own sword, but Brie knocked it to one side.

Looking up, Tabby saw King Gorgonzola

still standing by the stone bowl. He was whispering his wicked spell, over and over. *But where's Buddy?* Tabby saw him hiding behind a rock. His tail was curled up between his legs, and he was shaking all over.

"Come on, Your Dogginess!" Tabby called over. "You scared the rats last time!"

But the pup prince shook his head. "Now *I'm* scared! I can't sword fight. I don't even have a sword!"

"What a scaredy-pup!" laughed Brie. "Whiskered Wonders? Whiskered Wimps is more like it!" She pointed her sword so that Tabby had to duck again.

"Throw them in the bowl!" called King

Gorgonzola. "We will send them to sleep faster than you can say 'cheesecake'!"

The rats fought harder. Tabby was panting. Her paws hurt. *I don't know how long we can keep this up!* She saw Leo wipe his face. Felix's green eyes were wide with worry. Melted cheese was still spreading over the mountain, dripping and oozing between the rocks.

We have to do something . . .

Tabby looked again at Gorgonzola, holding the Orb of Plenty, silver and round like . . . like a ball. *That's it!*

She turned to Buddy. "Your Dogginess! Back at the palace, do you remember how we were going to play fetch?"

The puppy's ears shot up, and he jumped to his paws. "Oooh yes!" He gasped. "It's my favorite game."

"Well . . . fetch!" called Tabby. She pointed at the orb.

Buddy ran off like an arrow shooting from a bow. He raced across the mountaintop, jumping over rivers of cheese. His fur flew and his ears waved. He jumped into the air . . .

"What in the name of—" began King Gorgonzola.

But before he could finish, the pup prince dived over the top of the stone bowl. He took the Orb of Plenty between his teeth and landed behind the bowl.

"Nooo!" yelled King Gorgonzola.

"Noooo!" called the rats.

"Take that!" said Leo. He punched the air.

Buddy ran around the stone bowl and then back to Tabby. He took the orb from his teeth and passed it to her.

"You did it!" said Tabby. She put her arm around the pup prince's shoulders. "You're a real Whiskered Wonder!"

Chapter 9

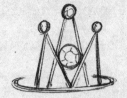

THE BEST DAY EVER

Gorgonzola pulled out his sword. He stomped toward Tabby, his face twisted with anger. "Give me back my orb, little kitty."

Tabby's heart was pounding. *I can't beat Gorgonzola in a sword fight.* But maybe there was another way. She turned around.

Gorgonzola laughed. "Running away, are you? That's not going to save you!"

Tabby felt around her skirts. *Come on,*

Tabby! A moment later, she was ready. "So you want the orb?" she called over her shoulder. "Here it is!" She flicked her paw.

Everyone watched in surprise as a shining silver ball flew through the air and—*plop!*—disappeared into the bubbling bowl of cheese. There was a hissing sound. Then the orb was nowhere to be seen. The other kittens and Buddy gasped.

King Gorgonzola laughed again. "You think that will stop us? Rats LOVE cheese!" He threw down his sword and ran to the stone bowl. Brie, Chedd, and Mozz raced after him. They all climbed up the side and jumped in together. *SPLASH!* A great wave of cheese spilled over the side.

Felix was chewing his claws again. "Oh my whiskers," he said. "Gorgonzola will have the orb back in no time!"

"Don't be so sure," said Tabby. She smiled and pulled a second silver ball from under her skirts.

Leo gasped. "Whoa! Is that . . . ?"

"It's the real orb!" said Tabby. "Gorgonzola is chasing after the fake cheese one. I had it hidden in my skirts all along."

"You tricked him!" said Felix, grinning. "Just like he tricked us."

"Exactly," said Tabby. "I suppose even these silly fancy clothes can be useful sometimes!"

The royal kittens and Buddy watched as

the rats splashed around in the big stone bowl of cheese.

"Where is it?" screeched Gorgonzola. His fur had turned yellow.

Mozz lifted up a cheesy bit of tinfoil. "Is this it?"

"Of course not, you fool!" yelled Gorgonzola. "And stop eating everything!"

Chedd and Brie were slurping huge gulps of cheese as they swam. Their bandanas had fallen off in the cheese.

"Sorry, Your—*gulp*—Stinkyness!" said Chedd. "It's so—*gulp*—yummy!"

Brie just blinked and yawned. *The cheese is going to put them to sleep!* thought Tabby.

Gorgonzola glared at the royal kittens.

"You'll pay for this!" He tried to climb out of the stone bowl. But the gooey cheese stuck to him, and he fell back in.

"He can't get out!" Leo giggled. "The cheese is turning solid!"

Sure enough, as the cheese cooled, it became thicker and thicker. The rats moved slower and slower. At last, they stopped moving.

"So . . . sleepy . . ." said Mozz. His eyes shut, and he began to snore.

"This is not over!" Gorgonzola yelled at the royal kittens. But he was so covered in cheese that all he could do was shake his fist.

King Gorgonzola's black nose rag had

come off, too. The rat gave a huge yawn, and his eyes closed. In an instant, he was snoring, too, belly-up in the cheese beside his three sleeping servants.

"You did it, Tabby!" said Leo, lifting his sword.

"*We* did it!" said Tabby.

"But it's not over yet," said Felix. "We have to get the orb back to the palace. And fast, or the party will be ruined!"

The royal kittens and Buddy ran all the way down the mountain. Tabby carried the orb in her paws, being extra careful not to drop it. *We can't lose it again!*

As they raced into the village, Tabby

saw sleepy cats and dogs getting to their paws, looking confused.

"Where am I?" said a dog.

"What happened?" asked a cat.

"Are those the Whiskered Wonders?" called another cat, pointing.

Tabby grinned and waved as they ran past. But there was no time to stop.

"We have to get to the Royal Avenue!" said Felix. He led them around a corner, and they came out onto the big main road.

The long table was almost ready for the feast. Kitizens were laying silver knives and forks on the white tablecloth while their new dog friends helped. But when they saw the royal kittens, they crowded around, patting them on the back and all speaking at once.

"I can't believe it. The Whiskered Wonders are real!"

"And they have the Orb of Plenty!"

"We have to get this orb to the end of the table," said Felix. "That's where Mom and Dad will be sitting. And we can't let them know we're the Whiskered Wonders!"

"I have an idea!" said Leo. "Let's roll it."

"Perfect!" said Tabby. She put the orb in the middle of the tablecloth. Then she gave it a push with her paw. The orb rolled along, down the table toward the palace. It began to slow down. But another kitizen helped it along with his paw. Then another pushed it. Everyone cheered as the orb passed by.

"Biscuits and bones!" said Buddy suddenly. "Mom and Dad will be missing me! We should run to the end of the table, too."

"No problem," said Tabby. "There's just one thing we have to do first . . ."

The four of them ran down a dark alley. Tabby led the way, turning a corner and racing to the goldsmith's shop. The shop was empty, but a window was open, and Tabby quickly untied her mask, sword, and cape and tossed them through. The others did the same.

Almost there, thought Tabby as they ran

down a long street and turned back toward the Royal Avenue.

There was a huge crowd around the end of the table. As Buddy and the royal kittens pushed their way through, Tabby heard a cheer go up all around. *The orb must have arrived at the palace!*

Puffing and panting, they climbed onto a small wooden stage and sat in the golden chairs placed there for them. King Pouncalot and Queen Elizapet were just lifting the Orb of Plenty up into the air for everyone to see. King Rover and Queen Ginger sat at their side, clapping their paws.

King Pouncalot gave the kittens a serious look, but Queen Elizapet seemed relieved.

Tabby knew they must have been wondering where their kittens had gone. She and her brothers took their seats between Captain Edmund and Nanny Mittens, who quickly licked a bit of Leo's hair back into place.

They looked out over the table. Cats and dogs were sitting side by side, smiling and cheering, as far as the eye could see.

"We made it!" whispered Leo.

"Let the feast begin!" said King Pouncalot and Queen Elizapet.

"*Orb of Plenty, hear my call.*

Show your magic, feed us all!"

Tabby grinned from ear to ear as every plate filled with yummy dog biscuits for the

dogs and hot fish pie for the kitizens. There were even a few tuna treats! The dogs and kitizens gasped and clapped. In no time at all, everyone was eating.

"Wherever have you been?" whispered King Pouncalot as he sat down.

"You made it just in time," added Queen Elizapet. "The Whiskered Wonders just brought the orb back and we almost had to start without you!"

"We're sorry—" Felix began. But just then, Buddy spoke up.

"It's my fault, Your Majesties," he said. "I wanted to play fetch. And the royal kittens were so nice and let me play with them. And I chased the ball. And then I caught the ball! And then I chased it again. And I've just had the best day ever!" He wagged his tail and gave Tabby a wink.

"Well, scratch my belly!" said King Rover. "It sounds like you youngsters are getting along very well."

Queen Ginger bowed to the cat king and queen. "If our pup and your kittens are such good friends, I see no reason why we can't be, too. Let there be peace between Mewtopia and Barkshire . . . forever!"

"Forever!" agreed King Pouncalot and Queen Elizapet. All four royals lifted their cups in the air.

Felix leaned over and whispered to the others. "Gorgonzola's wicked plan failed."

"The Whiskered Wonders have saved the day," said Leo. "Again!"

"But we couldn't have done it without you," Tabby said to the pup prince. "You're a hero, Your Dogginess!"

"Do you really mean it?" Buddy covered his face with his long ears. But even though he was shy, Tabby could tell he was smiling. "Don't worry," he said when he lifted his ears again. "Your secret is safe with me. Ooh, I wonder if that mean old rat will ever wake up and escape from that cheese. He looked really stuck, didn't he? Do you think he'll cause any more trouble?"

I wouldn't be surprised, thought Tabby.

She had a feeling that they had not seen the last of King Gorgonzola. But she wasn't afraid anymore. "I know one thing for sure," said Tabby. "If he does, the Whiskered Wonders will be ready for him!"

Don't miss Princess Tabby's next quest!

KITTEN KINGDOM
#3: Tabby and the Catfish

King Pouncalot threw out his paws. "Let the Peace Parade begin!"

A brass band began to play, and the kitizens meowed excitedly.

"There's one good thing about being stuck on the bank," said Felix. "We get to see all the other boats in the parade!"

Sure enough, as the royal boat moved off, more boats came sailing behind it. The first was piled high with brightly colored balls of wool. The next was painted all white, and was a very strange shape.

"It's a milk bottle!" said Leo suddenly.

The royal kittens giggled at the sight.

"That boat looks even funnier than the milk bottle," said Felix.

Tabby looked down the river and saw a huge yellow lump floating on the water.

Nanny Mittens frowned. "It looks like a big smelly cheese boat!"

Cheese . . . Tabby felt a shiver run down her tail. She looked at her brothers. Leo frowned, and Felix started to bite his claws again.

"You don't think . . ." whispered Felix. "It can't be . . ."

"King Gorgonzola!" finished Leo.